The Adventures of Mooli
and the Sticker Trickster

Asha Nehemiah is a popular author with children of all age groups. Wonderfully funny characters get into hilarious adventures and crazy escapades in her stories. *The Mystery of the Secret Hair Oil Formula*, *The Mystery of the Silk Umbrella*, *Zigzag and Other Stories*, *Granny's Sari*, *The Rajah's Moustache*, *Trouble with Magic*, *The Adventures of Mooli and the Blue-Legged Alien* and *The Adventures of Mooli and the Bully on Wheels* are some of her published titles. Her books have been translated into Hindi, Tamil, Bengali, Assamese and Urdu.
Visit the author at *www.ashanehemiah.com*

Published by Scholastic India Pvt. Ltd.
A subsidiary of Scholastic Inc., New York, 10012 (USA).
Publishers since 1920, with international operations in Canada, Australia, New Zealand, the United Kingdom, India and Hong Kong.

For information regarding permission, write to:
Scholastic India Pvt. Ltd.
A-27, Ground Floor, Sigma Centre
Infocity-1, Sector 34, Gurgaon 122001 (India)

First edition: October 2019

This reprint edition February 2026

ISBN 978-93-8929-735-5

Printed in India at Shivam Offset Press, New Delhi

The Adventures of Mooli and the Sticker Trickster

ASHA NEHEMIAH

Illustrated by Niloufer Wadia

SCHOLASTIC
New York Toronto London Auckland
Sydney New Delhi Hong Kong

A MESSAGE FROM SCHOLASTIC INDIA

Mooli and Soups are back!

The new trickster in town is rather tricky and our dynamic duo is on the case again! Peppered with silliness and perfect comic timing, I'm sure this will be a great addition to your bookshelf

We're very excited to be publishing the third instalment of this series. Hope you like it as much as we do.

Shantanu Duttagupta
Publisher

For Ayaan,

who will have many 'Wayouts' adventures of his own

Contents

Brand New Trick

A telephone call from Mooli usually meant that he had thought of at least five new ideas! And these were always the craziest and most unusual ideas. But this time, when Mooli called his best friend, Soups, it had nothing to do with ideas at all.

'Soups!' Mooli sounded like he had been running very fast. 'Can you come to my house at once?'

'Hi Mooli,' said Soups, 'do you think "stretch" rhymes better with "fetch" or "edge"?'

'Stretch? Fetch? Is this about our "yoga poem" entry for *Wayouts*?'

'Yes. Isn't that why you asked me to come to your house?'

'Soooups! We cannot think about *Wayouts* just now. The animal people are here. Please hurry and come here at once!'

'Wait, what animal people?' Soups was confused.

'Those people who fight against cruelty to animals. They are saying that Amma is being cruel to monkeys. Appa is not at home. So it's up to us to save Amma.'

This sounds serious, thought Soups. In fact, it sounded downright scary. Mooli not having the time to think about *Wayouts* was an EMERGENCY. Who were these animal people? And why did

Mooli's amma, Aunty Gita, need to be saved from them?

Supriya George (Soups for short) and Murali Krishnan (better known as Mooli) usually spent every minute, whenever they were not in school, thinking about how they could win a prize on *Wayouts*.

It had started during their summer holidays earlier that year. Soups' dad, Mr George, had told the children about a very unusual website called *Wayouts*. It stood for **W**orld's **A**s **Y**et **O**riginal **U**ntried **T**ricks and **S**tunts. *Wayouts* was something like a book of world records but also different in many ways. To begin with, being a website, it had to be read on the computer and not from a book. To win a prize, a person didn't have to do something faster or better than others. She or he simply had to do things that had NEVER been tried before. And that meant the stunts had to be ORIGINAL.

This is what a page from *Wayouts* looked like:

First Prize: Junaid Saleem, the juggler who plays the drums using only juggling balls, not drumsticks.

Second prize: Anika Henkel who sailed the river on a raft she made entirely from empty soft-drink bottles.

Mooli and Soups had sent thirteen entries to *Wayouts* but they hadn't won a prize yet. They were working hard on their newest entry—the yoga poem. It was very important for them to win this time. Their parents had told them that they could send

in ONE last entry to *Wayouts*, and no more. After that, they would have to stop trying out tricks and give up all their stunts.

Just one more entry! And here was Mooli saying he didn't have the time to think about *Wayouts*. Soups had to reach Mooli's house urgently.

Monkey Trouble

Mooli's house was very close to the apartment block where Soups lived with her parents. The children were allowed to walk to each other's homes on their own, but, as a rule, they had to inform their parents first.

Soups' dad, Mr George, worked from home. He was a genius who wrote all sorts of very complicated programmes on his computer. This meant that NO ONE was allowed to disturb him when he was at work.

DO NOT KNOCK!
DO NOT COME IN EVEN
IF A TIGER HAS
ENTERED THE HOUSE.
KNOCK ONLY WHEN
YOU CAN SMELL THE
TIGER'S BREATH.

On his door was a poster that said:

> *Do not knock! Do not come in even if a tiger has entered the house. Knock only when you can smell the tiger's breath.*

Soups thought for a moment. This was definitely more urgent than a tiger entering the house. So she knocked on her dad's door.

'I'm coming with you,' her dad said when Soups explained why she had disturbed him. 'This sounds like a load of fun.'

'Dad, this is not fun. This is serious. Mooli called me again and said that the animal rights people had started waving banners and were shouting angrily in front of his house.'

'I'll take you on my cycle then. Hurry!' They both grabbed their cycling helmets and rushed out.

All Soups and her dad could see when they first reached Mooli's house was a group of angry people waving banners that read 'Be kind to animals'. Then, they spotted Mooli and his amma, looking totally shocked. They were standing in front of the board that Mooli's Amma had put up right next to their house, just two weeks ago. The board read:

Cooked perfectly!
Yummy Scrummy
mon Keys
Pick them up here →

Next to the message was an arrow pointing to the side door of Mooli's house. 'Yummy Scrummy Monkeys! How did this happen to your board, Gita?' asked Mr George.

'Who changed your board like this, Aunty Gita?' Soups had to shout to be heard.

Mooli's amma, Gita Krishnan, ran a business called Yummy Scrummy Home-made Treats. She made and sold the most delicious cakes, biscuits and other wonderful treats. She ran her business from home and had just put up the new board to advertise it.

Mooli didn't like to see his amma looking so worried. He wanted to help in some way. But for once, he was out of ideas. While he thought of a plan, Mooli did what he was best known for—he fiddled. He fidgeted. And … he MEDDLED.

Animal Treats

'Soups, look!' Mooli was excited. 'It's only a sticker pasted onto Amma's board, see?' He was already busy picking the loose edge and peeling the sticker off.

Mooli's habit of meddling had earned him the nickname of 'Meddling Mooli', and today, his meddling fingers had made a very important discovery.

Very quickly, he and Soups peeled off the entire sticker with the word 'monkeys'

Cooked Perfectly!
mmy Scrummy
me-made Treats
K THEM UP HERE
monKeys
BE KIND TO ANIMALS
CHEF

on it. Now everyone could read the original message. It read:

Cooked perfectly!
Yummy Scrummy
Home-made Treats
Pick them up here →

'Someone stuck this on the board!' laughed Mooli, as he showed the sticker to the animal rights people. Amma hugged him. 'I know I always scold you when you meddle. But today, I'm truly thankful for your meddling ways. You saved the situation. Well done, Mooli.'

The people carrying the banners laughed. 'It's only a trick,' said one of them.

'It's a wicked trick by some mean sticker trickster.' Amma sounded very upset.

'Are you the person who owns Yummy Scrummy Home-made Treats?' The animal rights people sounded calmer already. And when Mooli, who had run into the house, came back with a tray of his amma's home-made butter biscuits for them, their mood changed faster than they could say 'monkeys'.

Once the banner-waving people left, the children, Amma and Uncle George went into the house. Soups' mother, Aunty Nirmala, joined them ten minutes later. She was a professor at a medical college that was quite close to Mooli's house. All of them sat around enjoying freshly baked treats still warm from the oven.

'Luckily, those animal rights people didn't come into your kitchen,' said

Soups, wiping crumbs off her chin. 'They certainly wouldn't have liked to see that you actually DO have fried monkeys and baked crocodiles on your kitchen counter. They're delicious!'

'Mmmm . . .' was all Mooli could mumble, his mouth filled with the warm, cinnamon 'crockies' (cookies shaped like crocodiles). 'Good thing I decided to hand out your butter biscuits instead of these.'

'How is it that all your treats are animal shaped this time?' Aunty Nirmala asked. She couldn't choose between the 'pupcakes' (cupcakes in a variety of dog shapes) and the 'monkey-knots' (doughnuts shaped like monkeys). So she took two of each.

'It's for an animal-themed birthday party for a child,' Amma explained. 'All the snacks and the birthday cake are animal shaped. Here, try some "roareos",' said Amma. The cookies were in the shape of a lion's face and sandwiched together with different flavours of cream.

'What on earth are the two of you doing now?' asked Uncle George, looking at Soups and Mooli. The two were sitting on the floor, each with a plate piled high with treats.

'Mooli, you look like you are about to be choked by that wire you are twisting around that rolling pin. And Soups, the little pieces of the newspaper that you are tearing up are flying into my milkshake.'

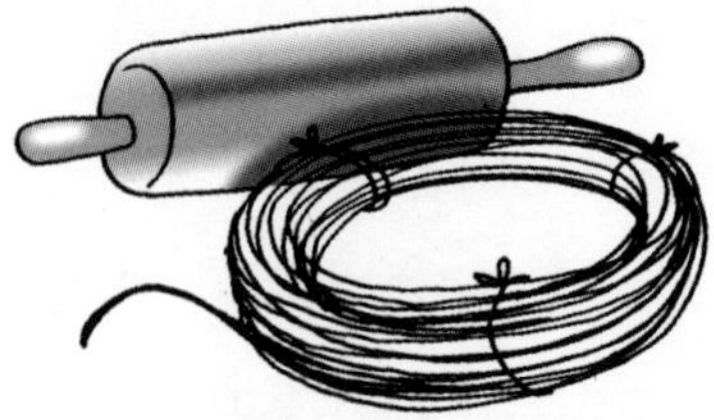

The Mooli Trap

'Mooli is making a wire sculpture from a single piece of wire using only cooking tools,' Soups explained. 'He can't cut the wire or use anything other than cooking tools to bend and shape the wire. He's making a dinosaur!'

'Soups is working on something that's even more difficult. We've called the trick "free-hand tearing to create art from a single sheet of newspaper". Look, Soups is not using scissors! She hasn't even drawn outlines of the shapes. Err … what's that scene you're tearing out, Soups?' Mooli had to ask because he couldn't recognize a single shape.

'I'm tearing out an underwater scene with submarines, octopi, fish and sharks. All the shapes are linked together, see? They're not separate. It's really tough to tear them out like this!' Soups held up the sheet for everyone to look at. The pile of torn newspaper next to her proved just how difficult this stunt was.

'But why are you both trying two separate stunts?' Aunty Nirmala asked. 'Remember, you are allowed only one more entry to *Wayouts*.'

'Err . . .' Mooli's amma looked guilty. 'Well, you know how I am always complaining

THE DAILY
HEAVY RAINS
CITY ROADS
BANK ANNOUNC
FREE
SPORT
JUDGE DECLA

about Mooli's meddling habits …' she said, lowering her voice '… and how annoyed I get when he can't stop meddling with things.'

'Like the time he tried to help you in the kitchen and mixed up the lids of the flour, baking powder, salt and icing-sugar jars,' said Aunty Nirmala, laughing. 'That was the time the cake you made turned out as hard as a brick topped with salty icing. Mooli always does something unexpected!'

Looking at the two heads bent over their work—one with a mop of curls and the other with straight silky hair—both mothers smiled.

'I was so relieved when Mooli pulled off the sticker, and proved to everyone that I wasn't being cruel to animals,' said Amma. 'And then he won them over by offering them my freshly baked butter biscuits. That was such a good idea!

'So I told the children that we would allow them to make just one more stunt entry, in addition to the yoga poem … for helping us sort out the problem with the animal rights people. Besides, these are not totally new tricks. They'd started working on them earlier. Now, they are working hard to finish them, before I change my mind,' she explained.

'Look at them. *Wayouts* keeps them so busy. I don't think they'll look up even if I light a firecracker right next to them,' Aunty Nirmala commented.

Half an hour later, it was not a firecracker but Mooli's appa who made all of them jump with fright.

Mooli and Soups were refilling their plates when Appa walked into the house. Just as he entered the dining room, there was a crash followed by a series of loud yells. Appa had tripped over the wire dinosaur. He ended up scattering the pile of newspaper pieces as he fell, and the wire dinosaur now circled Appa's foot.

'OH MY GOSH! What sort of a trap is this?' asked Appa, trying to free his foot. But the more he tried to pull his foot out, the tighter the wire sculpture seemed to grip it. 'I've never seen a trap like this before!' exclaimed Appa.

'It's a Mooli Trap,' said Amma, who couldn't help laughing.

Once Appa's foot was rescued from the trap, Mooli swept all the newspaper

CHEF
MONEY
NEWS
NEWS

bits into the dustbin, and Soups put the single-wire dinosaur sculpture carefully on the bookshelf.

'There!' she said, 'No one can trip over this now.'

Trouble Again

Soups was wrong, for the very next morning someone got caught in the trap again. And this time, it was Mooli himself! The wire dinosaur had fallen on the floor at some point during the night and the next morning, a sleepy Mooli tripped over it. He knocked the dustbin high into the air when he lost balance and a shower of newspaper pieces followed, with some pieces falling on a batch of freshly iced pupcakes. The dustbin flipped in the air and finally landed on Mooli's head.

No.1
NEWS

'Oh no, Mooli! What have you done to my pupcakes?' Amma was distressed. 'Ravi, I need help,' she said turning towards Appa. 'Can you, please, carefully remove the paper bits from the icing? I should start packing the rest of the treats for the animal-themed party's delivery.'

'I'm sorry, Amma,' Mooli said. 'I got up early because today is the day we are filming our yoga poem. Soups will be here soon. There, that's probably her now,' he added when the doorbell rang.

It was Soups indeed, and she had some bad news for Mooli and his parents. There was a crowd of people outside their house again, she said. She grabbed Mooli's hand and the two of them ran out together.

Amma followed, looking very worried. In her hurry, she forgot about the box of pupcakes she was holding and carried it outside with her. Appa followed close behind her.

Outside, there was a big crowd gathered around Amma's board. Luckily, this time, the people were laughing rather than being angry.

Soups, Mooli and his parents looked at the board in horror. It now read:

Cooked perfectly!
Yummy SMELL Y
Home-made Treats
Pick them up here →

'There's nothing smelly about whatever you're carrying in that box, Gita,' said one of the neighbours. 'It smells delicious!' Mooli's amma handed over the whole box

to the neighbour, much to his surprise, and walked up closer to the board.

'It's just another sticker,' said Mooli. His quick fingers were already trying to pry the sticker off.

'The wicked sticker trickster has struck again!' said Amma. 'But why would anyone want to trouble me like this?'

This time, the sticker seemed to be stuck more firmly than before. Though Mooli tried his best, he just couldn't remove the sticker from the board. He ran back into the house and returned with two butter knives from their kitchen and handed one to Soups.

'I've seen this sticker somewhere before,' said Soups as she helped scrape it off. 'It looks familiar. Now, where have I seen it?'

Soups had an amazing memory. Though she was only eight years old, she was already on her school's quiz team. She could answer questions that no one else could—not even the senior students.

'Think hard, Soups,' Mooli said. 'We need to find out why someone is doing this to Amma's board.'

Amma and Appa were walking back to the house, discussing whether they should take the board down, as it was causing a lot of trouble.

Before they could finish scraping off the sticker, Soups remembered where she had seen it before. She got so excited telling Mooli all about it that neither of them noticed they had scraped off some of the letters on the board. It now read:

Cooked perfectly!
my   crummy
Home-made r ats
Pick them up here →

Cooked Perfectly!
my crummy
Home-made r ats
PICK THEM UP HERE

'We have to catch this sticker trickster who is playing pranks on you, Amma,' said Mooli, once he and Soups were inside the house. He told his parents that Soups remembered where she had seen this type of sticker before.

'Finish filming your yoga poem first,' Amma suggested.

'Amma is right, Soups,' said Mooli. 'Let's finish our entry for *Wayouts,* and then we'll start looking for the prankster. We'll start from the street where you saw the stickers.'

Yoga Poem

Appa left to deliver the party treats and the children got everything ready for filming the yoga poem. Mooli swept the bits of torn newspaper back into the dustbin while Soups cleared some space to spread out their yoga mats.

Amma was going to shoot the video using her phone's camera. Usually, it was Uncle George who filmed the children's stunts. Each entry to *Wayouts* had to be accompanied

with a video clip, or a photograph, or a letter from a person who had actually seen the trick or stunt being performed.

Soups and Mooli had spent weeks practising the yoga poem, which they had written themselves. Each word of the poem was acted out using yogasanas that looked like the letters of the alphabet. They got their performance perfectly right on the third try, after which they gathered around Amma to check out the video.

'That looks awesome!' said Soups as she pressed the replay button. They watched the video five times. The video looked so wonderful that they decided to head to Soups' house immediately. They wanted Uncle George to send their entry to *Wayouts* at once!

'This is our best trick so far! Much better than the "single-squeeze toothpaste art" we had tried the last time,' Soups said excitedly as she and Mooli walked to her house.

'Or our stunt with the globe and arrow when we ran into the blue-legged alien,' added Mooli.

'I'm sure we are going to win a prize this time!' Soups said.

'Yes, the video of our yoga poem is looking really fantastic,' Mooli agreed. 'I am going to stop working on that wire dinosaur. It looks quite scary and dinosaur-like but the yoga poem is so much better!'

'I'm saving the newspaper from which I created the complete underwater scene,' Soups decided. 'Just in case.'

When the children reached Soups' house, they were thrilled to find Uncle George was taking a break from his work.

Soups and Mooli waited impatiently as Uncle George first watched the video a few times. Then, he praised the children several times. Finally, he made milkshakes for all of them before sending off the entry to *Wayouts*. Now that the entry had been sent, it was time to go searching for the sticker trickster!

At first, when Mooli and Soups reached the street where Soups remembered seeing the stickers, they thought she had made a mistake. They couldn't spot a single sticker. Not on the glass windows of the stores. Not even on the walls which were covered with posters of all shapes and sizes.

AVEL
CAFÉ
OPEN
PUSH
DUPLICATES FOR HOUSE, OFFICE, SAFE, CARS, BIKES
Happymon Keys
Keys to match any lock
Open 24x7
HONEST JOBS ONLY
WORK FROM HOME
Make more than your paycheck
Call me at 98010 09876
BlissLife
TOURS & TRAVELS
Destination Events
Package tours
Business tours Expert
MATHS TU
BEST RESULTS 2019

'No stickers in sight! Just posters advertising Zoom-Zoom Zumba, Swalpa Salsa Dance Company, Diva Perfume Spray, Centum Maths Tuitions, Happymon Keys … such funny names!' said Mooli as he read them aloud.

But before he could read out any more posters, Soups suddenly clutched Mooli's arm.

'I've found the sticker trickster ... right there!' And she pointed to one of the posters.

Setting the Trap

Mooli looked carefully to where Soups was pointing, but couldn't spot the trickster anywhere in the poster. Soups laughed and then read out loud, '"Diva Perfume, smell your best all day". That's where the word "smelly", stuck on Aunty Gita's board, comes from. Remember how there was a small gap between "smell" and the letter "y"? That's because the word "smelly" has been cut out from two different words—"smell" and "your".'

'And this is probably where the word "monkeys" comes from,' Mooli guessed, pointing to the poster with the words 'Happymon Keys'.

And right then, Mooli's meddling fingers made another amazing discovery. 'The glue used to stick the Diva Perfume poster seems just as strong as the one used to stick the word "smelly". It's impossible to pull this poster off!' he said.

'And the Happymon Keys poster is just as easy to pull off as the word "monkeys"!' Soups found out. 'What we need to do now is catch this trickster in the act of sticking the words that change the meaning on Aunty Gita's board. But how will we do that?'

'Quite easily. We just have to use our trap!' Mooli grinned. 'We'll put our wire-dinosaur sculpture right next to the delivery board and hope that the trickster doesn't notice it.'

Mooli's idea worked splendidly.

The next morning, it was still dark outside and Mooli was fast asleep when a loud shriek jolted him awake. Mooli's parents were up already as Amma had started her morning baking. Mooli jumped out of bed and ran outside, with his parents following close behind.

In the dim early-morning light, they could see someone lying sprawled on the grass, caught in the trap. The small bucket of glue with a brush and a pile of torn paper pieces from posters was all they needed to confirm that this was, indeed, the sticker trickster.

Amma helped the culprit stand up, and as Mooli wrestled with the wire to free the trickster's foot from the trap, they got their first proper look at the sticker trickster. She was a young girl, probably about eighteen years old.

'My … ouch … name … oow … that hurts … is Richa …' she said between yelps of pain.

OUCH!

Amma took the girl inside the house while Mooli quickly gathered up the torn poster pieces and dumped them into the bucket of glue. The single-wire dinosaur, their 'trap', was now completely out of shape, so Mooli threw that into the bucket as well and carried it inside.

Once they went in, Amma gave Richa the best cure she knew for pain—a tall glass of milkshake and a plate of chocolate-filled roareos.

The Trickster's Story

The cookies worked magic on the painful foot and soon Richa was telling them her story. She was a college student, she said, and was always looking out for part-time jobs to earn a little pocket money.

'Putting up posters is boring, but the timings suit me well. However, there is a big problem. People hate these posters because they spoil public spaces. So they tear them down. When that happens, I don't get paid.

'Last week, a wedding catering company—which supplies food at weddings—asked me to put up posters advertising their business. These are the same caterers who order wedding cakes from you, ma'am,' she said, turning to Amma.

'I put up their posters one morning, but every single poster was torn down by the next. That's when the owner of the catering company gave me an idea. He told me that any glue I used for sticking the posters had to be so strong that your son, Mooli, wouldn't be able to remove it. He said that was the only way I'd get paid for putting up the posters. So, I worked out this plan. I'm sorry I changed the words on your board by sticking words cut out from the posters. It was the only way I could test the glue; by making sure that Mooli wouldn't be able to tear off whatever I had stuck.'

They all peered into the bucket of glue. It was now a colourful mix of paper bits; mostly different shades of green, as the pieces had been torn from a poster advertising organic spinach.

Amma seemed to like Richa, so she made her an offer. 'Well, Richa, since you are looking for part-time work, maybe I could offer you a job. I've been looking for someone to help me with the delivery of orders at Yummy Scrummy Home-made Treats. So, would you be interested in taking up a part-time job with me, delivering cakes? Whenever you have some free time on your hands?'

Richa was delighted! She couldn't believe her mischief had got her a job.

The deal was struck in the best way possible, with all of them tucking into some cake—warm and fresh from the oven.

Then Richa apologized to Amma. 'I'm so sorry. I hope I didn't cause too much trouble for you. It was very thoughtless of me.' She stopped and looked at the bucket of glue. 'I'm never going to use this glue again. Where shall I put it?'

Mooli offered to show her. Seeing the dustbin filled to the brim with newspaper bits, he emptied those into the bucket of glue as well. He didn't want any more accidents with the dustbin and newspaper even though his wire-dinosaur 'trap' was now safely in the bucket, covered with glue, bits of poster paper and newspaper.

'Mooli, I have a question ... why were you making this deadly trap?' Richa asked, pointing to the dinosaur sculpture. And so, Mooli spent the next five minutes talking about his favourite topic—*Wayouts*.

'You'll be meeting my friend Soups soon. She's coming over to meet you. You see, we had expected the sticker trickster to look far more mean and wicked.'

And just then, the doorbell announced Soups' arrival.

Disappointment and Chocolate

Some news is best shared over triple-chocolate cake—a chocolate cake with chocolate chips and chocolate icing—and this was that sort of news.

Many days later, the Krishnan family and George family were meeting for Sunday lunch. Uncle George had called Amma earlier and warned her about the 'news', so she had made chocolate ice cream as well.

Uncle George waited until they had all eaten a good amount of dessert before breaking the news. 'Soups, Mooli, I think your yoga poem performed in yogasanas was the best, I mean the absolute best trick or stunt that the two of you have done so far.' He stopped to clear his throat.

'Yaay! Yipee!' Soups and Mooli started jumping excitedly.

'But wait. There are these twin sisters from Thailand, seventy-seven years old—not that age matters—who performed a yoga story. An entire story that they had written, performed in yogasanas. And what's more amazing is that they performed their yoga story underwater, wearing scuba-diving gear and oxygen tanks! So, their yoga story beat your yoga poem to win the prize on *Wayouts.*'

Mooli was so disappointed that he felt as though the chocolate cake had

suddenly turned to wet mud in his mouth. Soups looked calm, but when she put the chocolate ice cream into the pickle jar instead of her bowl, everyone knew she was upset too.

'Well, we still have one try left,' Soups finally spoke up after all of them had eaten their ice cream in silence. 'Mooli, where is the single-wire sculpture of the dinosaur? You could still finish that. And I'll complete the underwater scene I was working on. We'll decide which of the two tricks to send to *Wayouts* once we are done.'

'My wire sculpture has been pulled completely out of shape. It looks nothing like a dinosaur now,' Mooli replied.

'Well, I've kept my underwater scene that I tore out from a single sheet of newspaper,' said Soups. 'You remember how well that had turned out, Mooli?'

Mooli broke into a wide chocolatey grin. Soups smiled back thinking Mooli had suddenly remembered how wonderful her underwater scene was. Actually, Mooli was trying hard not to laugh thinking about the bunch of unrecognizable shapes that Soups had torn out from the paper. But he didn't want to hurt her feelings because Soups was always kind to him. She always helped him with his maths homework, never once laughing when he made a mistake. So all he said was, 'You know what, Soups, I still have quite a lot of wire left. Let's take a look at the old dinosaur sculpture, but I'll probably have to make a new one. And maybe, this time, I could use a different set of tools …

instead of Amma's rolling pin,' said Mooli sheepishly, looking at Amma. The last time he had used her rolling pin, Mooli managed to lose it and it had made Amma angry.

It took them a little while to find the single-wire dinosaur. It was still in the bucket of glue, next to the garbage bin. Luckily, the dry garbage for that week had not been collected yet.

The glue, with the bits of green paper and newspaper, had hardened into one big mess. Most of it was a muddy-brown colour but there were lots of shreds of bright green too, from the poster advertising organic spinach.

Success at Last!

'This looks nothing like a dinosaur. I can't make out its head from its tail!' said Soups in dismay when they took the wire sculpture out of the bucket. 'I can hardly *see* the wire! It's all coated with glue and paper.'

'Yes, this scary dinosaur looks just like a pile of dried grass now. And these bits of green paper look like fresh grass growing on it,' said Mooli, as he turned the sculpture around in his hands. 'But surprisingly, it's still very flexible.'

'Hmm, it may be flexible, but there's no way we can pass it off as a sculpture,' Soups decided.

'Don't worry, Soups. I'll just start again. Come on then, let's go find the bundle of unused wire.' Mooli left the mess of wire and paper and glue at the foot of the steps. He'd throw it out later, he thought.

'And I'll find my underwater scene when I go home,' Soups sounded more cheerful as they walked up to Mooli's room. They had barely reached the top of the steps when they heard a loud shout. They rushed down to find Appa with his foot caught in their dinosaur sculpture … again!

'It may be useless as a dinosaur sculpture, but it still works well as a trap,' said Appa rubbing his foot. 'In fact, it works really well as a trap because it looks as harmless as a pile of dry grass or straw!'

'Are you two thinking the same thing that I am?' Uncle George asked the children. Soups and Mooli didn't answer. They were already busy discussing how to word their new entry to *Wayouts*.

Pictures were taken. Then the trap was taken outside, placed on the grass and Uncle George took a video of Mooli's amma getting her foot caught in the children's latest entry to *Wayouts*. It was a dangerous trap, cleverly disguised to look as harmless as a bit of dry grass. It was made from a single length of wire, shaped using only cooking tools and finally finished off with a single dip into a pail of glue and waste paper. Now, *this* was truly original!

Just on
BUND
FLOO
SPOR
Floods

Two weeks later, Amma put up a poster on her board; the same board that she had been meaning to take down. The poster read:

Neighbourhood Animal-themed Party!

To celebrate

Supriya George and Murali Krishnan

Winning a prize on Wayouts! →

Under the message, strung up with a ribbon, was their prize-winning entry to *Wayouts*.

There were wonderful treats to eat and lots of party games. When the guests finally left after having a great time, Soups and Mooli helped their parents clear up.

'Hey, why are you throwing away your entire underwater scene?' Mooli asked

Cooked Perfectly!
Yummy Scrummy
Home-made Treats

Soups, seeing her dump the sheet of newspaper into the trash.

'Now that we've finally won a prize on *Wayouts*, don't you think we should try something different?' Soups asked.

'Yes. Something totally different would be fun,' Mooli agreed.

'I've thought of two good ideas already,' Soups' eyes were shining. And as Soups shared her ideas, several new ones popped into Mooli's head.

By the time they reached the front door, the two best friends had thought of at least seven new ideas. All *original*, *untried* and wonderfully *different*.

OTHER BOOKS IN THIS SERIES

The Adventures of Mooli and the Blue-Legged Alien

Winner of the Best in Indian Children's Writing (BICW) Award 2019

Mooli's (Murali Krishnan) meddling ways usually get him into trouble but he also has some of the best ideas.

Soups (Supriya George) loves reading and is super-smart. The best friends are on a mission together to win a prize on a cool new website, *Wayouts* (**W**orld's **A**s **Y**et **O**riginal **U**ntried **T**ricks and **S**tunts)

They try the most unusual stunts and even track down a Blue-Legged Alien. Is that enough for them to win the prize?

The Adventures of Mooli and the Bully on Wheels

Shortlisted for the Neev Book Awards 2019

Mooli and Soups are still on their mission to win a prize on *Wayouts*. Their tricks and stunts get more creative than ever and they have a rollicking time. They create paintings from toothpaste, draw maps with spaghetti and meet a bully intent on stopping them.

Do Mooli and Soups manage to outwit the bully and finally win the prize?

OTHER BOOKS BY ASHA NEHEMIAH